Tenggren's
Pirates, Ships, and Sailors

by Kathryn and Byron Jackson

pictures by Gustaf Tenggren

 Golden Press · New York
Western Publishing Company, Inc.

CONTENTS

Pirate's Cove 9

Stowaway Judy 13

Old Captain Garrett 16

The Careful Cheerful Sailor 18

Pirates' Glen 21

The Wonderful Bottle 22

Storm at Sea 25

Orders is Orders 26

Seafaring Tommy 29

The Flying Dutchman 30

Twenty-five Sailors 32

The Rescue of the Sea Cow 34

The Stubborn Stubborn Sailor 37

The Icebound Ship 38

The Big Little Cook's Boy 39

In the Sea an Oyster 43

Fog Horns 43

Long-ago Toby 44

Seagulls 46

Widow Harper's Spice Cake 47

The Whale, the Whale 50

Rainy Day Sailboat 52

The Sad Sea-cook 54

Sea Serpents 56

Mutiny 57

Lighthouse 61

Pirate's Cove

PIRATE'S COVE was a wonderful place to live in during the summer. There was the bright sea for a boy to swim in, and the curved white beach shaped like a brand-new moon. There were the cliffs, and the rolling hills to play on and explore.

Best of all, there was the name Pirate's Cove.

Pirate's Cove! Kit could close his eyes and see a great pirate schooner rocking in the harbor. He could see its black flag blowing against the blue sky. Sometimes he could even see a band of pirates coming ashore. They rowed in, shouting and singing, with their peg legs, and eye patches, and a heavy chest of treasure to hide at the Cove.

And who knew—perhaps the pirate treasure was still there! Who knew—maybe a boy could find it!

"If he searched long enough, and dug deeply enough," thought Kit, "maybe a boy my size could find a chest full of old pirate gold!"

Kit even thought the boy might be himself! So he got a shovel for digging and he took his flashlight for looking in holes. He took a chocolate bar, in case of sudden hunger, and his best pistol, just in case.

Then Kit went out, and every day he dug in a different place.

He dug under trees that looked like good landmarks. He dug holes in the beach, and at the edge of the cranberry bog. He dug in likely places and unlikely places.

And one day Kit dug up a rusty lantern. He ran home with that.

"Does it look like a pirate lantern?" he asked his father.

"No," said his father. "It looks like it might be an eel fisherman's lantern."

That's what it was. It belonged to old Silas Prentiss, who was glad to get it back.

And one day Kit found a skull.

"Does it look like a pirate's skull?" he asked his father.

"No, it doesn't, Kit," his father said. "It looks exactly like a sheep's skull."

Then he said, "You know, Kit, pirates roved the sea over a hundred and fifty years ago, and I think you're wasting your time. I think you'd be better off learning the crawl or rowing your boat."

"Is that orders," asked Kit, "or is it up to me?"

"It's up to you, Kit," his father said. "But I'd like to see you playing on the beach."

The next day Kit practiced his crawl. He rowed his boat up the cove. The water sparkled. The sunshine was warm on his head.

"My father was right," he thought. "This is fun. I like this."

He watched a seagull soar lazily toward the hill. Its shadow slid across the beach, then along the cliff. Suddenly the shadow disappeared. Kit looked sharply at the cliff. There was a hole in it, right where it met the water. A hole like the door of a cave.

Kit swung his boat toward the beach. He rowed to shore and dropped overboard the big stone he used for an anchor. He ran across the beach and waded along the face of the cliff to the cave.

Kit's heart was beating as loudly as the sea. He peeped into the cave. It smelled of seaweed,

9

and damp, and salt. It was dark in there. Kit turned on his flashlight and crept in. The cave was big inside. He could stand up.

"Even a pirate could stand up in here," he thought. And when he said "pirate," he was sure this was the hiding place. There were rocks all about, damp rocks that shone in the flashlight beam.

One by one, Kit moved those rocks. But there was no hole under any of them. So he walked around the cave, searching the walls.

At last he found a loose rock. He pried it with his knife, and it came out. Kit reached into the hole.

"There's something in it!" he shouted.

"—in it!" called a hollow voice back in the cave.

Kit jumped—then laughed a shaky laugh. The voice was only an echo!

He reached into the hole and brought out a rusty box.

"It's a mighty small box for a treasure," he thought.

He opened the creaking lid. Oh, gosh, there was no ruby in it, no big perfect pearl, not even a very small diamond!

There was a paper in it. A folded, heavy piece of paper.

Kit took it out into the sunshine. At first it looked blank, the sunshine was so bright. But then Kit could see lines and numbers and letters on it.

"A map," he whispered. "It's a treasure map!"

It didn't take Kit long to get home. He found his father under the car talking to himself. Kit wriggled under, too.

"Look, Daddy," he said. "Look at this! Does it look like a pirate's map?"

"Pirates!" his father growled. "Here, hold this wrench, Kit."

At last his father said, "There, I have that leak fixed."

He shoved himself out from under the car and sat on the grass. Kit flopped down beside him and gave him the paper.

His father looked at it and whistled. Then he shook his head and frowned.

"Kit," he said, "somebody's teasing you. Everybody in the Cove knows you're treasure hunting. Somebody hid that map for you to find."

Kit gulped.

"Are you sure, Daddy?" he asked. "Are you certain sure it isn't a pirate map?"

Kit's father nodded.

"Certain sure," he said. "Look, it says, 'From the bent tree, an hundred paces due east in line with the turtle back—' "

"Yes, I see," Kit said. "What's wrong with that? What's a turtle back?"

"It's the island with the lighthouse on it," Kit's father said. "Looked like a turtle before they built the lighthouse."

He pointed to the old tree that leaned over the cliff.

"You see, Kit, if you went a hundred paces from the tree—you'd be out in deep water."

"Oh," sighed Kit. He sounded like air going out of a balloon.

His father patted his shoulder.

"Never mind, Kit," he said, "when I get the car running I'll take you down to the post office. We might stop for a soda, too."

"Yes, sir," Kit said. "First I'd better get my flashlight. I left it in the cave."

But once he was in his boat, Kit could not get straight to the Cove. He looked up at the bent tree, and he looked out at the lighthouse on the turtle back.

He rowed his boat in a straight line between the two. And every few feet Kit stopped and looked down into the clear water of the Cove.

He saw little snappers darting into the shadows. He saw an eel and a horseshoe crab. He saw the green seaweed waving on the white bottom of the cove.

And then all at once, Kit saw a place where the white bottom did not show. It looked like a shadow. Kit's small head could not make a shadow that big. Kit leaned way over the side and looked down.

He leaned a bit too far, and the boat tipped, and Kit fell into the water with a great splash.

"Ugh!" spluttered Kit when he came up.

Then he laughed at himself.

"Pretty clumsy, pretty clumsy! But now that I'm in here, I'm going to see what that dark patch is on the bottom!"

He swam down as far as he could, and he looked still farther down. There was a big green rock down there. There was something else.

It looked like a boat. It looked like a funny kind of boat. Just what kind, Kit could not see. He had to go up for air.

When he came up, his small boat had drifted away. Kit started to swim for it. But somebody called, "Hello, Kit!"

It was his father. He was coming toward the boy in his motorboat.

In a few seconds, Kit was beside his father in the launch.

"I said practice your crawl," his father said sternly, "but I didn't say, 'See if you can swim to Spain'!"

"I fell out of my boat," Kit panted. "I was looking at a hundred paces due east, and Daddy, there's a boat down there—it's a funny boat—"

Just then Kit remembered his own boat. It was drifting out toward the sea.

"Look, Daddy!" he shouted. "It will get lost!"

It didn't take long for the motorboat to catch Kit's rowboat. Kit jumped into the water again and tied it to the stern of his father's boat. His father swung him aboard.

"Can we go look at that sunken boat, Daddy?" he asked eagerly.

"You just bet we can," his father said. He spun the wheel. Kit pointed the way.

Together the two leaned over the side and looked down at the green shadow.

"Does it look like a pirate dinghy?" Kit whispered.

His father did not answer. He was kicking off his shoes. He grabbed a rope and put it around his waist. Then he dived down into the clear water.

When he came up, Kit asked again, "Does it, Daddy?"

His father took a deep breath. "Thought we could tow the boat ashore. But the wood is rotten. The boat has been there too long."

"Has it been there a hundred and fifty years?" Kit asked eagerly.

"Maybe it has," his father said.

Then he dived down a second time. When he bobbed up again, he flung the end of the rope to Kit, and climbed into the boat.

"We'll soon see, Kit," said his father.

He pulled and pulled on that long rope. Pretty soon Kit could see a dark shape coming up through the water. It was squarish. It looked green. It looked like a large box all green from being in the water.

Kit did not ask any questions now. His father reached into the water and lifted the dripping box into the boat.

"It's light, Kit," he said. "It's too light to have much in it."

He put his knife under the rusted lock and broke it open. Together Kit and his father looked in. A hole had rusted in the bottom of the box.

"Whatever *was* in it is gone now," Kit's father said. Now *his* voice sounded like an emptying balloon.

But Kit reached into a corner of the box.

"Look, Daddy!" He held up an old darkened coin.

His father felt and looked at it, and rubbed it in the sand in the bottom of the boat.

"It's a gold coin, Kit!" he shouted.

And before Kit could say one word, his father had dived into the water again.

At last he came up, panting hard and dripping. "There's nothing else down there," he said.

He picked up the one gold coin and turned it over and over in his hand. Then he gave it to Kit.

"Well, Kit," he said. "There's your pirate treasure. The rest has long ago been washed out to sea. Not a chance of finding any more of it."

"Is it *really* pirate gold?" Kit asked.

His father nodded.

"Sure enough," he said. "It's a real Spanish doubloon. That old box must have been full of them at one time. It's a pirate treasure chest, certain sure."

Kit looked at his wonderful Spanish doubloon. He looked out at the shining water.

"An hundred paces due east," he whispered happily.

So the big pirate schooner really had anchored in the cove, and the pirates really had rowed toward shore with their peg legs and eye patches, and a big chest of treasure to hide at the cove!

Yes, Pirate's Cove was a wonderful place to live in during the summer. Pirate's Cove! Who knew but what there was more treasure somewhere? So much that the pirates had not bothered to bring up the small chest in the dinghy boat that sank? And who knew but what a small boy might find it?

"A boy just my size," Kit murmured.

"A boy just your size had better get on some dry clothes if he wants to go to the village with me," his father said.

And side by side, both dripping wet, they rode slowly in toward the curved white beach that was shaped like a brand-new moon.

Stowaway Judy

JUDY WATCHED the seven trim sailboats practicing for the big race. All of them looked beautiful scudding down the gray bay. But Judy thought the one with the big blue "3" on its sail was the best of all. That was because its name was *Judy*, too, and it was her father's boat.

"The *Judy* is out in front!" she squealed.

But Billy Ames and Stevie weren't listening to her. They were too busy talking about sailing. They talked about tacking and reefing and sailing into the eye of the wind.

Billy said, "Golly, Steve, in two years I can help sail my father's boat!"

"I'm going next year," said Stevie. "Next year I'll help sail in the big race. Golly!"

Judy shouted, "Golly, Billy! Golly, Stevie! The *Judy* is still out in front!"

But they just nodded and went on talking.

Judy kicked at the green, slippery moss on the jetty. She tugged at Billy's pocket.

"I'm going this year," she said in a loud voice. "I'm going to help in the big race this year!"

Billy and Stevie both looked at her in surprise. "You're never!" cried Billy.

Stevie said, "You're only six!"

Judy tossed her head.

"Just the same, I'm going!" she said.

Her heart began to bump so hard she couldn't stand still. Judy knew her father hadn't said she could go. She knew she had better say, "I was only fooling," right away.

But Billy and Stevie looked at her as if she were just as big as they were.

"Are you, honest-to-goodness?" they asked.

Judy crossed her fingers inside the pockets of her dungarees. She nodded her head. Then she ran down the slippery jetty and back home as fast as she could go.

That night she tried to ask her father if she could go on the race. But her father looked very big and stern with his tanned face and bright blue eyes. Besides, he was busy talking to her mother. He was talking about tacking and reefing and sailing into the eye of the wind.

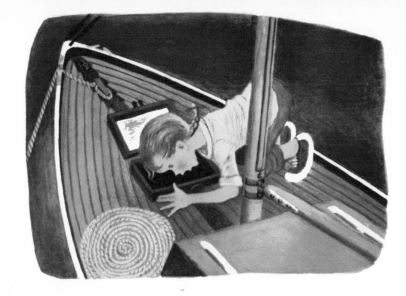

Sailing was all he talked about for days and days. Whenever Judy tried to ask if she could go along, he said, "Don't interrupt, Judy." Or else Mother said, "Judy, you mustn't talk when your mouth is full!"

And whenever Judy tried to tell Billy Ames and Stevie that she wasn't really going, the words would not quite come out.

At last it was the day before the race. Judy climbed down on her father's boat while it was tied to the dock. She ran her hands over the hot shiny deck, and felt the warm, coarse canvas sails. She sat cross-legged in the cockpit and pretended.

"Now it's tomorrow," Judy told herself. "Now the race is going to start, and I'm going along—"

She opened the little doors into the rope locker. There were coils of rope in there under the deck. But there was lots of room besides.

"Room enough for me to stow away!" whispered Judy.

She thought she could hide in there early in the morning and be there during the race.

"When the race is over," she thought, "I could crawl out and hop up on the dock. And then Billy and Stevie would see that I really truly did go along!"

Just before supper, Judy hurried down to the sailboat again. She put a pillow in the rope locker, and a box of crackers. She put a bottle of lime soda in the middle of a coil of rope. Then she put her lucky rabbit's foot under the pillow.

"Now the *Judy* is sure to win the race," she whispered.

And just after she had backed out of the rope locker, her father came down to the boat.

14

"Mother wants you to set the table, Judy," he said.

Judy ran home. She set the table and washed her face and hands. She never interrupted once when her father was talking. And right after supper, Judy said good night.

"Don't you feel well, Judy?" her mother asked.

Her father didn't say anything. He looked the way he always did when he was going to tell a joke. But he didn't tell one.

He just said, "Judy has a lot on her mind." Then he said, "Good night, Judy."

Judy was curled up in bed before it was nearly dark. She closed her eyes and listened to the water sloshing against the jetty. The sailboats were all rocking on the bay, now. Their sails were folded. They were rocking and waiting for tomorrow.

"If only I can wake up early enough," Judy whispered. In two minutes she was sound asleep.

When she woke up, it was so early that nobody else was awake. Judy scrambled out of bed, dressed in a wink, fixed her own breakfast, and tiptoed down to the dock.

She crawled into her stowaway place and pulled the doors closed—all but a tiny crack.

The waves lapped against the bottom of the boat and sounded nice and cool. But the sunshine beat down on the deck. Judy's hiding place got hotter and hotter. It smelled tarry from the rope. And Judy heard a tiny crackling noise that sounded like a mouse nibbling at her crackers.

She began to think her father would never come.

And just as she thought that, he jumped down into the boat. It seemed to rock much more wildly under the deck than it ever did on top! Suppose, just suppose, the *Judy* turned over in the race!

Now Judy didn't want to be a stowaway any more. She wanted to crawl out of the dark hot little locker, and away from that much-too-close mouse. But she remembered Billy Ames and Stevie. She lay perfectly still and closed her eyes.

"I'll stand it, somehow," she told herself.

And then her father said, "All right, Judy, come out of there. I intended taking you along all the time—"

Judy poked her head out of the little door.

Her mouth made a surprised O.

And her father, who was busy raising the sail, said, "Bring the crackers and the soda and the pillow and the rabbit's foot with you."

Judy gulped. "How did you know they were here, Daddy?" she asked. "How did you know I was stowing away?"

"A bird told me," her father said. "A hungry seagull."

He laughed as if he had told a dandy joke.

"The same bird told me that we're going to win this race, sailor," he said.

Just then the wind filled the sails. The *Judy* skimmed over the bright blue bay toward the starting line.

The racing course was miles long. All morning the sailboats sailed around and around the course. The *Judy* seemed to go faster and faster and

faster. When the race was over, the *Judy* had won. She won the big silver cup for being the fastest sailboat of all. And when at last Judy herself climbed out on her own dock, she had that splendid shiny prize in her two hands.

Stevie and Billy stared and stared at the cup. They said, "Golly, Judy!" over and over again. And they looked at Judy as if she were bigger than they were—and smarter than they were—and a real sailor, besides.

Old Captain Garrett

1. *Old Captain Garrett of Peabody Lane*
   Walked with a limp, and he walked with a cane,

2. *And he walked up the beach by the light of the moon*
   With a shovel all smooth at the tip, like a spoon.

3. *He dug in the sand with great vigor and pleasure,*
   And said he was digging for lost pirate treasure.

4. *All the people in the town heard him say it. They said:*
   "Poor old Captain Garrett's not right in the head!"

5. *But once on an evening quite foggy and drear,*
   Why, old Captain Garrett, he cheered a great cheer.

6. *"I've found it!" he cried. "The lost treasure I sought!*
   And I've doubloons all golden, for things to be bought!"

7. He went shopping next day for wonderful things:
   Scarlet coat, and a sash, and big golden earrings.

8. And a sword, and a knife, and a black pirate hat.
   And he paid for them all with his treasure—like that!

9. Oh, he made a strange sight as he strutted about
   With his limp and his sword and his loud pirate shout,

10. And his queer pirate clothes, and his bags full of gold.
    But the people in town (so the story is told)

11. Bowed and smiled as he passed.
    And they asked him to tea.

12. They said, "Captain Garrett's as smart as can be!"

17

The Careful Cheerful Sailor

AND ONCE THERE WAS a careless ship that sailed carelessly with its sails full of holes and its hold full of rats. Nobody knew what the cargo was. If you asked the captain, he said, "I don't know. I didn't notice," and went back to reading his comic books.

But the cargo was heavy and the ship had a list. It leaned way over sideways, and when the sea was rough it leaned over so far that the waves washed the decks with sudsy foam. That was just as well because the sailors never had washed the decks and never would.

Even if the captain had looked up from his comic books long enough to say, "Sailors, ho! Wash the decks!" the sailors would have said:

"No, we don't want to wash the decks. We don't care if they are dirty."

And nobody knew where the careless ship was going. Nobody cared. Even if you had asked the pilot where it was going, he'd have scratched his head and said:

"I forget. Maybe we're going to latitude and maybe we're going to longitude. I don't care where we go, anyway."

He never went near the helm and never looked at the North Star or shot the sun, which was very careless in a pilot.

All he did was wish he were back in London eating sugar buns with currants.

But there was one careful sailor on the careless ship. He had a dreadful, busy time but he was always cheerful, nonetheless.

He mended sails until his thumb was numb.

And he spliced ropes until all the ropes were spliced into one rope.

He looked at the North Star every night.

And he shot the sun every single day.

He went to the helm at lunch hour and turned the wheel until the ship *looked* as if she were going some place, anyway.

He washed the dishes in the galley.

And he made a trap to catch the rats. It wasn't a very good trap for rats but it did catch the second mate when he went in the hold to steal some jam.

And whenever he sat down, that one careful sailor always sat on the high side of the listing ship to try and weigh it down even with the low side.

But one careful sailor can't take care of a careless ship. Oh, no—it takes a whole crew to keep a ship in shape.

So one day, when a storm blew up and the rain rained in sheets and the wind blew in furies and the sea rose up and down like a whale with the whooping cough, the careless ship was thrown up in the thick gray air. It came down sails down. It rolled over full of water and it couldn't right itself because of the list, and so down it went, down and down into the slate-gray sea.

Bubbles came up . . . bubbles and bubbles.

And the captain came up with his comic books, and the pilot came up with his "I don't care," and the first mate and the second mate and all the careless crew.

They tried to swim but the waves were very rough. And they saw the one careful sailor in a neat lifeboat, rowing away with two neat oars. He had a tin of dry biscuits and a keg of clear water and every chance of reaching the mainland or at least an island of some sort.

But all the careless sailors and the captain and both mates climbed into that little lifeboat.

It went down—

And down—

And down—

until all you could see was a lot of frowsy heads, and one tidy head, bobbing in the rough sea.

They bobbed for quite a while.

A seagull came and said, "My goodness, this is dangerous!"

And a porpoise came and said, "What's dangerous about it?"

And when everybody was very tired of bobbing, a ship sailed up.

It was a tidy ship, with a careful captain who liked everything shipshape.

He saw the bobbing heads through his well-polished spyglass and he slapped the gleaming rail and cried:

"Man the lifeboats!"

The crew knew their duty. They let down the

19

boats and rowed out to the bobbing heads. They pulled the careless captain and his careless crew out of the sea.

And the one careful sailor climbed out himself.

But when the bos'n of the careful ship saw that careless crew, he threw up his hands.

He looked at the careless captain and his wet comic books and he said, "Tut, tut, we can't rescue him! He bites his nails and our captain can't abide nails that are bitten!"

So he threw the captain, comic books and all, back into the sea.

And he couldn't save the pilot with his tousled hair.

Over went the pilot.

One by one the tidy bos'n observed the careless crew.

"None of them will do!" he declared. "Too careless. Holes in socks, showing toeses. Dirty faces, runny noses. Missing buttons, dirty nails! We never could clean them. We haven't the pails for a job like that!"

He looked very sorry but he said, "Throw them back!"

All the careless crew went back—"Splash!"—into the sea.

"What about me?" asked the one careful sailor with his cheerful smile.

The bos'n grinned a friendly grin and clasped the sailor's nice clean hand.

"You're just the man we want," said he. "Our captain will be glad to see such a tidy, shipshape sailor."

The captain was. He beamed with pleasure when he saw the sailor.

"This ship needs a careful mate. I fancy you will do first-rate—you tidy, careful sailor."

And the tidy sailor came to be the Admiral of the King's Navy—after several years, of course, and after many sailings and scrubbing decks and polishing railings.

He wears a neat three-cornered hat with ostrich feathers pressed out flat and a long blue coat with golden braid.

He's a splendid figure on parade.

That careful, cheerful sailor!

20

PIRATES' GLEN

Go shouting up the cobbled hill
   But whisper in the glen—
You never know when you may meet
   A band of pirate men!

It's true. They came here long ago
   With chests of pirate stuff.
You never know what we may find
   If we dig deep enough.

We might find ropes of oyster pearls
   Or heaps of gold doubloons,
Or gold from Madagascar, or
   A chest of silver spoons.

Or maybe ancient treasure maps
   Or diamonds by the ton,
Or cutlasses with jeweled hilts
   Or—just a skeleton!

Or—just around that darkish tree—
   Did you hear something crack?
The pirates might be coming now
   To get their treasure back!

Let's hurry up the ferny hill
   And not come back again.
I don't believe I want to meet
   A band of pirate men!

The Wonderful Bottle

ONCE THERE WAS a little girl who went to the seashore for the first time. She stayed there all summer long, and that was a wonderful summer.

On sunshiny days the little girl played at the edge of the sea. She paddled her feet in the little waves, and when they ran out, she looked to see what they had brought to shore.

They brought seaweed that popped when you pinched it, and strange shells and beautiful shells, and starfish that were hard as stone when you let them dry in the sun.

And on rainy days the little girl put on her rubbers and put up her umbrella and went for a walk up the cobbled hill. Halfway up she turned around and looked down at the harbor. It was full of ships that rocked and swayed in the rainy wind on the wet sea.

Then she went on, up and up the steep hill. And at the very top of the hill there was a small shop. The little girl stopped there and looked and looked and looked in the window.

That window was only as wide as the little girl was high, but it was full of the most wonderful things. There were small figures carved of wood: sailors and whales and a splendid sea serpent, and a bold pirate with one peg-leg. There were conch shells that give back the sound of the sea, and there were starfish.

And then there were ships.

The ships were tiny, but they looked just like the real ships in the harbor. Some were on small wooden stands, and one, the most beautiful ship of all, was in a bottle. How it ever had gotten in, the little girl could not tell. The neck of the bottle was much too small for it to pass through.

She wanted very much to go into the shop and ask about that ship. But the old sailor inside never looked up. He had a stern and lonesome look, and he always seemed very busy. He was whittling away, and if you went in he might say, "Go away, little girl. I'm busy. Can't you see how busy I am, little girl?"

So the little girl did not go in.

She just stood outside in the drip-drip-drip of the rain and looked at the wonderful bottle.

And then one day in the middle of the summer, this little girl was far up the beach watching sandpipers, watching sand cobblers, and she saw something bobbing in the shallow water. In she went— and out she came with a bottle in her two hands. It was a long bottle, flat on one side. It was as clear and green as a wave breaking in the sunshine. And it was a wonderful bottle just like the one in the window of the shop.

Now the little girl did not wait for rain.

She went straight up the hill in the sunshine, up to the top.

A bell tinkled when she opened the door of the shop. And when she put the wonderful bottle on

22

the counter, the old sailor looked at her and smiled.

He didn't say he was busy.

And he didn't say, "Go away, little girl."

What he said was, "This is a splendid bottle for putting a ship in!"

He began at once to make a little ship. He carved the hull just the size to go through the neck of the bottle, and he painted it dark, deep red.

That was all he did that day, and the little girl went home.

But the little girl went back the next day and the next. Every day for days and days the little girl watched the old sailor work. He carved tiny masts and cut tiny sails. He made tiny ropes and ladders of linen thread. He painted all the parts with clear paint that was shiny.

It took a long time to finish that little ship.

And at last the day came when the little girl had to go back to the city.

She went to the beach and said good-by to the seagulls and the starfish and the strange shells and the beautiful shells and the seaweed that popped when you pinched it.

And then she went up the cobbled hill to say good-by to the old sailor and the wonderful bottle and the little ship that was not quite finished.

But when she went into the shop, the old sailor held up the ship with its folded sails.

"Now we'll put her in the bottle," he said.

He pushed the little ship through the neck of the bottle, right to the middle. Then he pulled on the threads that were looped about the masts.

Up they went—masts, sails, ropes, and all—and there was the ship all finished. There it was inside the bottle, and looking too big to have gone in!

The sails seemed full of wind, just as if the ship were sailing on a real sea. And the little girl saw that there really was water in the bottle.

She sniffed, and the water smelled salty like the sea.

She shook it a little, and the salt sea water tossed in tiny waves.

"It's the most wonderful bottle and the most wonderful ship in the whole world," the little girl said.

And then it was time for her to go.

She thanked the old sailor for letting her watch, and hurried to the door.

But the old sailor called her back.

"Aren't you going to take your bottle, little girl?" he asked.

The little girl leaned way forward.

"With the ship inside?" she whispered.

"With the ship inside," said the old sailor.

He put the wonderful bottle in her hands.

He said it was hers to take back to the city.

Then he began to whittle away, and he would not look up when the little girl thanked him. He would not look up when she went out the door and the bell tinkled. He would not look up so she could wave good-by. He just sat in his little shop whittling away, and the little girl went down the hill.

She took her bottle home to the house by the sea—

And home to the apartment in the city.

She put it on the window sill in her own high-up room. And there it is every morning when the little girl wakes up. A tiny ship, in a wonderful sea-green bottle, sailing on a real little sea.

So the little girl never did say good-by to the most wonderful part of that wonderful summer, after all.

Storm at Sea

IT WAS a rainy, stormy, blowy day outside. "But it's snug inside," said the old sailor. He took a grandchild on each knee.

"Storms," he said. "I've seen storms. Aye, I've seen a storm come up all at once—the sky went black as pitch. The sea rose up in waves like walls, and our ship bobbed and bounced on them like a rubber ball.

"The deck was awash like a waterfall. The wind howled and the ship creaked and complained just like you've been doing. The rain came down in sheets. You couldn't stand up for the rolling of the ship. You couldn't sit down for the mates' crying out orders. You couldn't get dry. All the clothes on the ship were soggy wet, and the air itself was wet. Even the sea biscuits were wet and soggy.

"Why, we couldn't even eat in peace!

"The plates danced off the table, and the potatoes hopped out o' their skins and rolled up and down the cabin. The knives played mumblety-peg all by themselves. And the ship's cat clung to a swinging lantern and swung to and fro."

The old sailor stopped for a moment and listened to the sound of the wet wind. Then he nodded his head.

"Aye," he said to the children. "You talk about storms! You've never seen such a roaring storm as I've seen. And then, all at once, I've seen the sky brighten and the sun come out. The ship settled down on the smooth sea, and the storm was over. . . ."

He pointed out the window, and both children looked.

"Aye," called the old sailor, "The storm's over, but 'twasn't your creaking and complaining did it. Remember that next time it rains, you hear?"

But the children were gone. They were out on the beach, running along the bright wet sand.

The old sailor laughed.

"Seems to me I recall creaking about storms myself," he said.

He picked up a torn fishing net and went out into the sunshine to mend it. And he sat in the brightest, warmest spot, as if he never had gotten all the salt sea damp out of his sailor clothes.

Orders Is Orders

ONCE THERE WAS a little boy who lived with his aunt in a little house close to the sea. The white sand was in front of his house, with tufts of tall tough grass in it, and in front of the sand was the ocean. At first the ocean was shallow with flat little waves that spread out of the sand. Then it grew deeper with splashing waves that had white, sudsy foam on top. It grew deeper and deeper until it was so deep that nobody knew how deep it was, except one old whale and one or two sailors on the big ships out on the deep sea.

The little boy watched those big ships while his aunt gathered cockles and mussels alive, alive-o.

He thought he would like to be a sailor on a big ship. And he watched the ships so hard, and thought about being a sailor so hard, that when his aunt said, "Briny, lad, help me gather cockles and mussels alive, alive-o," he only half heard her.

That made his aunt shake her head.

One day, when she was shaking her head and gathering cockles and mussels alive, alive-o, the little boy went up to the little attic of the little house. He found an old trunk in the attic.

In it there was a fine sailor's spyglass that needed polishing—

A jacket and trousers that needed buttons—

A sailor's hat that wanted a new ribbon—

And a sailor's log, which is not a log at all, but a book in which sailors write down what they do each day.

The little boy polished the sailor's spyglass, and sewed buttons on the sailor's suit, and put a new ribbon on the sailor's hat. He wrote his name in the sailor's log.

Then he tried on all the sailor's clothes. They were quite too big for him, but he wore them just the same.

"Aunt," he said to his aunt, "I'm off for to be a sailor."

His aunt stopped shaking her head and nodded it instead.

"Aye, lad," she said, "I thought you would soon be doing that."

She went back to gathering cockles and mussels alive, alive-o, and the little boy walked straight to the harbor and to the biggest ship in the harbor. It was a long walk.

He asked to see the captain.

"Well, lad," said the captain, "what can I do for you?"

The little boy said, "I have a polished spyglass, a sailor's coat with buttons, a sailor's hat with a new ribbon, and a sailor's log with my name on it. Now, what I want is to be a sailor."

The captain looked very serious about being a sailor.

"Do you know how to obey orders?" he asked.

"What is that, please, sir?" asked the little boy.

"It's doing just exactly what you are told to do," the captain told him. "Do you do that?"

Now the little boy thought. He thought he would like to say "Yes" but he knew he could not. He knew he never did obey orders when his aunt said, "Briny lad, help me gather cockles and mussels alive, alive-o."

So he said, "No, sir. I don't."

The captain looked stern. "Well, then," he said, "you certainly can't be a sailor on my ship."

The little boy gulped. He took out his sailor's log with his name in it.

"Please, sir," he said, "if you'll give me your name and address I will put it in my log book. Then when I learn to obey orders, I will come to see you again."

"Fine," smiled the captain, "fine. But remember, one order isn't orders. Two orders aren't orders, either. You take orders until your sailor's suit and your sailor's hat fit just right. Then come to see me."

He gave the little boy his name and address. It was Captain Josiah Retort on board *H. M. S. Fearless*. The little boy wrote that in his log book.

Then he went home. That was a very long walk.

He put his sailor's spyglass and his sailor's suit and his sailor's hat back in the old trunk in the attic. But he kept his sailor's log under his arm.

Down to the beach he went, to find his aunt. She was very busy gathering cockles and mussels alive, alive-o.

"Briny lad," she said, "help me gather cockles and mussels alive, alive-o."

"Yes, ma'am!" said the little boy.

He set right to work and gathered lots of cockles and mussels.

They tasted very good for supper in a sort of stew in a deep, green bowl.

And that night, before the little boy went to bed in his bed near a window where he could hear the big waves breaking into little waves and the big ship's horns telling each other where they were, he wrote in his log.

"Obeyed orders," he wrote.

He wrote that in his book every night until he was so big that his sailor suit with buttons and his sailor hat with a new ribbon fit him just right.

Then he took his spyglass and his log book and went back to see Captain Josiah Retort on board *H. M. S. Fearless*.

The captain looked in the log book full of "obeyed orders." He smiled. He shook the little boy's hand and said, "Now you may be a sailor on my ship!"

A sailor's life suited the little boy to a T.

He climbed up riggings—

And polished brass—

And battened down hatches.

He obeyed orders as fast as they were given.

He saw storms and strange foreign lands and he even saw the one big whale who knew how deep the ocean was.

"That is something worth writing in my log book," he said to himself. So he did. He wrote about seeing the whale on page 762.

He wrote about it to his aunt, too.

She was very pleased to get that letter.

She read it twice upside down and three times upside up. It seemed to make better sense that way. Then she put the letter in her pocket and patted it.

And then she went back to gathering cockles and mussels alive, alive-o.

SEAFARING TOMMY

1. *Tommy's a seaman on cleaning-house day.*
    With a mop and some soap and a pail,
    He swabs the front porch, and the steps to the yard
    Till they shine like the back of a whale.

2. *Tommy's a captain on washing-clothes day.*
    When the wash blows out white on the line,
    He sails in a basket just under the sheets
    For the sailing on Monday is fine.

3. *Tommy's a pirate on baking-things day.*
    When warm cookies are piled on a plate,
    He creeps down the stairs where the shadows are deep
    And he takes some for pieces of eight!

29

The Flying Dutchman

OLD CAPTAIN GARRETT liked very much to tell stories. He told about storms and whales and cannibal islands. And do you know, in every story he ever told, he was swallowed whole, or drowned dead, or cooked to a turn in a cannibal's pot!

A very wonderful man he was, and all the children on the beach listened to his tales with open mouths.

"Did I ever tell you about me and the Flying Dutchman?" he asked one day.

The children shook their heads and came close.

"Well, sir," said old Captain Garrett, "I'll tell you right now . . ."

And this was his story:

It was a fine day, so fine that I had to whistle at my work. I was a young man then, very brave and marvelous, and a capable second mate.

I said to the first mate, "Well, sir, fine weather behind us, fine weather ahead of us. A prosperous voyage, and we'll be home on time or my name's not Garrett."

The first mate straightway clapped his hand over my mouth.

"Man!" he cried. "That's no way to talk. Your boasting's enough to tempt the Flying Dutchman to pursue us!"

Now, I had heard tell of the Flying Dutchman. A ghost ship she was supposed to be. Aye. The story

went that she would come at a ship head on— and if the ship turned so it wouldn't hit her, why, it would surely be wrecked on rocks or reefs.

But I took no stock in the tale. A ghost ship! Who would believe such nonsense?

I laughed it off with a hearty, "Ho, ho, ho!"

But even as I laughed, the blue sky went black! A terrible storm came on us, sighing and roaring. Rain poured down like a wet wall, and our good ship tossed like a matchstick.

"See what you've done, man!" the first mate shouted.

And no sooner had he said that than the storm stopped as if it had never been. No wind blew. There was no sound on all the sea. But a heavy white fog hung about us, thick and woolly. I could scarcely see my own hand. Then suddenly, out of the silence, a fog horn sounded.

It set me shivering, I can tell you!

"Ship ahead!" whispered the first mate, and he swung the wheel to port.

Whooooooooooo! Whooooooooooo!

The horn sounded to port!

Again the first mate swung the wheel. Again and again he turned the ship. But no matter what way he turned, that horn sounded just ahead.

Suddenly the fog lifted for a moment. Straight toward our bow came a great dark ship. She seemed to swoop down on us, and on her bridge stood a strange, pale captain. He pointed one bony finger right toward me!

"It's the Flying Dutchman!" the first mate hissed. "You tempted her with your boasting! Now we'll all perish on some fearsome rocks!"

Closer and closer came the wild dark ship. The first mate made to turn the wheel. But I put my hand on his arm.

"Sail straight at her," I begged.

Then I ran down from the bridge and hurled myself into the sea. Down I went, deep, deep, into the dark water, never to come up again.

And even as I did, the fog disappeared. The sky and sea were fair and blue. The Flying Dutchman was gone. But on each side of our good ship loomed jagged rocks. Another turn of the wheel

and she would have crashed into them and sunk!

"Alas for the man who gave his life to save our ship!" sighed the first mate. "Alas for poor, brave, wonderful and marvelous second mate Garrett!"

Oh, all my shipmates were sore grieved that I had drowned to satisfy the Flying Dutchman! But I never regretted it, nor do I to this day.

Now old Captain Garrett took a big, dark bar of tobacco out of his pocket, and bit off a piece, and chewed away.

He looked out to sea with a dreaming look that meant he would tell no more stories that day. And the children ran off to play at the edge of the sparkling sea in which the wonderful, brave, and marvelous captain had drowned so many times!

TWENTY-FIVE SAILORS

1. *Twenty-five sailors went down to the sea.*
   One was the first mate. "Look lively!" said he.

2. *Two stowed the cargo down deep in the hold*
   And battened down hatches to keep out the cold.

5. *Five lighted lanterns, the red and the green,*
   And swabbed till the decks were all shining
   and clean.

6. *Four shoveled coal in the furnace of steel.*

9. *One was the captain—he tried the lifeboats*
   And looked at the buttons on twenty-four coats.

10. *Then toot! went the whistle.*
    Ding dong! went the bell.

And twenty-five sailors, as proud as could be,

3. *Three stored provisions to eat day by day.*

4. *Four made the bunks in a seamanlike way.*

7. *Three charted courses and tried out the wheel.*

8. *Two called the hour out, "Eight bells! Time to go!"*
   And pulled up the anchor with "Yo-ho-ho-ho!"

11. *Up the stack went the smoke with a fine*
    sooty smell.

12. *Out of the harbor, and out of the bay*
    The ship it went sailing away and away.

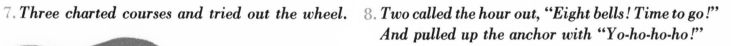

twenty-five sailors went sailing the sea.

The Rescue of the Sea Cow

TOMMY AND JIMMY lived in a lighthouse out on the deep blue bay. In the daytime they watched the ships go sailing by, and they played games on the salty rocks, and they watched their father clean the lamps in the top of the lighthouse tower. At night they listened to the waves and the bell buoys and the sound of the ship's horns.

Some ships whistled. Some hooted like old, old owls, and one had a deep, long horn that sounded like a cow saying moooooo.

The two little boys called that ship the *Sea Cow*. They liked that ship with the deep, long horn sound.

"I wish we knew which ship she is," they whispered to each other in the night in their round room in the lighthouse.

But they never could tell. Not ever.

When the ships went sailing by in the day, they did not blow their horns, unless it was foggy. And when it was foggy, Tommy and Jimmy could not see the ships at all.

One day it was sunny. The sky was high and blue, and everybody felt so good at breakfast that the lighthouse keeper laughed out loud.

"Mother," he said to his wife, "I'm going out to oil the bell buoys so they won't get rusty. You come along and bring your fishing line. It just might be that you'll catch a bluefish. Then we'll eat bluefish with lemon and butter for supper and a pie of canned blueberries."

The little boys' mother said, "Well, I don't know. What if a storm should blow up? What if a fog should blow in? Who would light the lamps so the ships would beware the rocks?"

The lighthouse keeper looked up at the blue sky. He thought of the bluefish and the blueberry pie and said:

"Tommy and Jimmy can be lighthouse keepers for today."

34

That made the little boys feel proud. They felt proud when their mother and father rowed away from the rocky island. And when the rowboat was only a speck on the blue bay, they felt very proud.

"We're the lighthouse keepers now," they said, and they didn't play on the rocks that day. They had to be sure everything on the island was just right. They looked in the rocky caves to be sure no pirates had come ashore in the night. They fed the seagulls the breakfast scraps. And they dusted all the rooms clean as a whistle, so there would be no dust to dim the lamps in the lighthouse tower.

Then they went outdoors again. They looked up at the sky. It wasn't blue any more. It was gray and thick.

The bay and the sea were gray, too. And a splendid big steamer was coming into the gray bay. Their father rowed up close to it. He seemed to be talking to an officer on the splendid ship. Then he sat down and rowed his boat back toward the rocky island just as fast as he could row.

But when his boat was halfway back, it disappeared! A fog had drifted in from the sea, a fog as heavy as a gray blanket. Then everything was still, except the bells on the bell buoys. They rang softly through the heavy gray fog.

"Halloooo!" called their father.

Tommy and Jimmy called "Halloooo!" But their father could not quite tell where the island was. The bells seemed to ring everywhere, and the two little boys' halloooo seemed everywhere, too.

Just then the little boys heard a deep moooooo, out on the foggy bay. It sounded near and far away both at once, and it sounded all around.

"It's the *Sea Cow!*" cried Tommy.

And Jimmy shouted, "Come on!"

Both boys ran into the lighthouse, and wisps of fog slipped in with them. They ran up and up and up the winding stairs into the high-up tower. Tommy climbed up to the lighthouse lamps, and Jimmy handed up the matches and the lighter.

"Hurry," he whispered. Tommy lighted all twelve lamps just as fast as he could. When they were all lighted, the great light shone out the windows. It shone out through the fog.

And the *Sea Cow*, much too close to the rocks,

blew its deep mooing horn and turned just in time. A minute later it would have been wrecked!

Now the boys' father saw the light and rowed straight toward it. Soon father and mother had landed at the foot of the lighthouse.

"You were good lighthouse keepers," the father told the two little boys at supper. He gave them each a big piece of bluefish and a bigger piece of blueberry pie. And after supper they went to sleep in their round room in the lighthouse, with the waves and the fog and the bell buoys all around and the light streaming out across the bay.

In the morning the fog was gone and the sky was blue. The splendid steamer that the little boys had seen the day before came steaming toward the rocky island. It was gleaming white, had lots of flags, and a name in gold letters on the bow.

The name was *The Queen of Columbia*.

But all at once that splendid ship blew her horn. And it sounded deep and long and low like a cow's moo.

"It's the *Sea Cow!*" whispered Tommy and Jimmy both together.

And then that splendid steamer dropped her anchor. An officer

with gold braid on his blue coat got into a small boat. Two sailors rowed him across to the rocky island. He climbed ashore and shook hands with Tommy. He shook hands with Jimmy.

"You saved my ship from the rocks yesterday," said the officer. "I came to thank you."

He gave them a long package, shook hands again, and went back to the ship.

In that package there were flags—four beautiful bright signal flags. Two were for Tommy and two were for Jimmy.

Their father showed them how to signal words to ships.

And ever after that, there was fun whenever *The Queen of Columbia* steamed across the bay. The boys, waving their signal flags, "talked" with the officer in gold braid on the bridge.

The Stubborn Stubborn Sailor

(Suggested by Irene Alleman)

1. Now once there was a sailor who
      Was very tall and thin.
   He always wore a raincoat and
      He always wore a grin.
   He always was found sitting
      In the still and sunny spots,
   A-trying hard as he could try
      To tie the sailor knots.

2. He said, "I'll tie a bowline, now,"
      And then, "I'll tie a reef . . ."—
   "A mooring knot . . . a half-hitch—so!"
      But always came to grief.
   For all his knots were knotted to
      His whiskers or his hair.
   (When shipmates tried to show him how,
      He said, "Shucks! I don't care!")

3. One day when it was foggy, all
      Around the rocking ship,
   He sat there tying knots, and sighing—
      "These knots—they seem to slip!"
   And when the cook called, "Chow time—chow!"
      A-banging on his pots,
   The sailor came with dolphin-leaps—
      He'd tied himself in knots!

37

The Icebound Ship

"ICEBERGS AHEAD!" shouted one sailor.

"Icebergs astern!" shouted another.

"Icebergs to port!" the first mate cried.

"Icebergs to lee!" shouted the crow's-nest watch.

"Icebergs everywhere!" thought the captain, rubbing his cold hands. "What to do! What to do!" he muttered, and he paced up and down the icy deck.

Then he shouted, "Sail between those two icebergs!" He pointed ahead at two mountains of ice far enough apart for the ship to sail through.

The ship sailed toward them. It sailed between them. And there it was, with a great iceberg on each side.

Suddenly, one iceberg started to get smaller—and the other iceberg began to get bigger!

"Ice is shifting!" shouted the crow's-nest watch.

"Full steam ahead!" the captain cried.

"Aye, aye, sir!" cried the engineer.

But it was too late. Those two ice peaks were part of one enormous iceberg with a shelf in the middle. Before the ship could pass, the shelf rose up from the sea—and the ship was sailing in an

icy lake with towering cliffs of ice all around.

"We're trapped!" the crow's-nest watch called.

"We're lost!" cried a sailor.

"We'll freeze!" the cook wailed, waving a pot.

"Or worse—" whispered an old sailor who thought he heard a rumbling.

In a moment, everyone heard the rumbling. Everyone heard an icy groaning and crunching—and then, with a tremendous loud CRACK! the ice shelf split right in two!

Cold green waves splashed up. Spray splashed up and froze the moment it hit the rigging. The ship bounced and bobbed and rolled in a strip of sea between two ice cliffs.

"Full steam ahead!" the captain shouted.

The ship raced ahead between the frozen cliffs.

Out it went into the open sea. Just as it did, one cliff fell CRASH! into the other cliff. Chunks of ice spun through the air. The cold sea tossed in great waves.

"Due south!" cried the captain.

The ship turned south and headed home.

"We're saved!" the crow's-nest watch called out, and all the happy sailors shouted, "Hooray!"

The Big Little Cook's Boy

THE GALLANT TAR was an enormous big four-masted schooner.

And all the sailors on the *Gallant Tar*, from the Captain (who was six feet nine) to the cook (who was six feet one), were big tall men with mustaches.

But the cook's boy was not big.

He was a wee bit of a boy.

At first all the big sailors looked way down at him and thought, "Avast! This wee bit of a boy is not big enough for our ship. We'll have to get a big boy in the next port."

The cook said it right out loud.

That made the cook's boy feel even smaller.

But the boy said to himself, "Great deeds make big men." That was something his mother had always told him. And he did his work as well as if he were six feet nine.

He peeled potatoes white and clean. He scoured pots until they shone, and worked his fingers to the bone keeping the galley shining. He set the tables for captain and crew, and never minded carrying stew to the men on watch when the sea was stormy.

Everybody on the *Gallant Tar* came to think that the cook's boy was a fine cook's boy.

"He's the best we *ever* had," they said.

And then, one dark and moonless night, a pirate ship slipped silently up alongside the *Gallant Tar*.

Twenty fierce pirates crept aboard.

They had knives in their teeth and pistols (the double-barrelled pirate kind) in their hands. They captured everybody on the *Gallant Tar* and lined them up on deck.

"Sailors," said the pirate captain, "I give you a choice. Either you can join the pirates and do just as I say—or I'll put you below IN CHAINS!"

All the sailors on the *Gallant Tar*, from the captain (six feet nine) to the cook (six feet one), said, "We are honest sailors, and we will NOT join the pirates and do as you say!"

But when it was time for the cook's boy to decide, he said to himself, "Below in chains I can't do any great deeds. Above and free, it may be that I can."

He said to the pirate captain, "I'll be a pirate."

But he kept his fingers crossed as he said it. Nobody noticed that. All the pirates cheered.

"Yo ho ho, and a dead man's chest,
This cook's boy seems to know what's best!"

The sailors of the *Gallant Tar* scowled at the cook's boy. Then they walked by him on their way to below-decks and to their chains without even looking at him. And they mumbled in their mustaches, "This cook's boy is a coward! He's the worst cook's boy we ever had."

The cook's boy tried to pretend he didn't care. He tried very hard to pretend he was a real bad, bloodthirsty pirate. He did just as the pirate captain said. Before long all the pirates thought he *was* a real pirate.

They asked his advice about where to bury their treasure. They let him decide who was the best knife thrower in the crew. They had him polish their guns and sharpen their knives, and they liked his cooking very much. And all the time the cook's boy was polishing or sharpening or cooking, he was trying to think up a brave plan for a great deed.

One night he thought up a plan.

The next morning he walked right up to the pirate captain.

"There's plenty of white chicken put down in fat in the ship's stores," he said, "and there's plenty of red wine in a moldy cask. Now, what I say is, why not let me cook an extra good dinner to celebrate your capture of the *Gallant Tar?*"

The captain grinned a greedy grin.

"A capital idea!" he roared.

And the other pirates sang:

"Yo ho ho and a dead man's chest,
This cook's boy sure knows what's best!"

The cook's boy cooked a splendid meal. He even made baked beans and pies. And he filled the pirates' plates and cups again and again and again.

The pirates ate until they felt stuffy, and drank the red wine until they felt drowsy. When they all had their chins on their arms, and their arms on

41

the table, the cook's boy brought in the pies.

"Wow!" said the pirate captain. "Wow!"

He cut the pies and passed big wedges all around. All that pie made the pirates sleepier than ever.

"It's time to take bread and water to the sailors in the chains below," said the cook's boy.

The pirate captain groaned. He was too stuffed to go below. He was too sleepy, too.

"You take it down," he said to the cook's boy. "Be sure to lock the door when you come out."

He gave his big key ring to the cook's boy. Then he put his head on the table and began to snore big pirate snores. All the other pirates put their heads down, too. And all twenty pirates snored—snore, snore, snore.

The cook's boy grinned.

He tiptoed all around the big table and took all the pirates' knives, and all their guns, which were the double-barrelled pirate kind.

He put them in a bag.

Then he slipped down below where all the sailors were in chains.

The sailors wouldn't even look at him.

But when the little cook's boy took out the key ring and unlocked all their chains—then they looked!

Their eyes were as round as the full moon. Their mouths were as round as port holes.

"Silence!" whispered the cook's boy. "Take off your boots and follow me up above. Quiet, now!"

He gave each big sailor a knife or a double-bar-relled pirate gun, and he led them back to the sleeping pirates.

All the big sailors crept

up on the pirates with their knives and guns ready.

"SNORE, SNORE, SNORE," went the pirates.

The sailors crept closer and closer, but still the pirates did not wake up.

"Pick them up," breathed the cook's boy, "and carry them below!"

And the big sailors picked up the twenty pirates. They carried them below and put them in chains. The cook's boy locked the locks and gave the key ring to his own captain who was six feet nine.

Then his captain and all the sailors and the cook went up on deck. They set the *Gallant Tar* toward home, where the pirates would be put in jail.

"—and most likely hanged," said the captain of the *Gallant Tar*.

He picked up the cook's boy and set him on his shoulders.

"Give three cheers for the cook's boy!" he said.

The sailors didn't need to be told twice. They threw up their caps and shouted, "Hip! Hip! HOORAY for the brave little cook's boy!"

They said, "He's the best little cook's boy we EVER had!"

And the cook's boy, up there on the captain's shoulder, was a good three feet higher than any of the big sailors on the *Gallant Tar*, from the captain, who was six feet nine, to the cook, who was six feet one.

He looked down and he smiled, and he thought to himself, "My mother was right when she said 'Great deeds make big men!'"

As for the pirates below in chains, all *they* said was: "SNORE, SNORE, SNORE!"

In the Sea an Oyster

In the sea an oyster
Makes a wondrous pearl,
And on the windy seashore
A ragged fisher girl
Wishes for a penny
To buy a sugar bun—
Wishes she had many.
(Pennies she had none.)
The sea turns and tosses
And tips the oyster bed,
And out rolls the oyster
Heels over head.
"Oh, what a pretty oyster!"
The fisher girl cries.
And when it is opened
She opens wide her eyes
And whispers and whispers,
"A king's ransom pearl!
I'll live like a princess,
A king's little girl!"

FOG HORNS

Sometimes at night when I'm in bed
    I pull the pillow round my head,
For fog horns on the big dark lake
    Cry out and keep me wide awake.
They take a breath and then they cry,
    With voices shrill or deep or high,
"W-H-H-H-O-O-O ARE YOU?"
    And "W-H-H-E-R-E AM I?"

But when I watch the lake by day,
    And all the fog has blown away,
And pilots on the lake can see,
    The ships move onward silently.
They look so proud and bold that I
    Can't quite believe I heard them cry,
"W-H-H-H-O-O-O ARE YOU?"
    And "W-H-H-E-R-E AM I?"

Long-ago Toby

THIS WAS all long ago.

Long ago, a little boy named Toby lived in a seafaring town. Almost all the fathers in the town were sailors. They went down to the sea in big sailing ships. And when they came back there was a great hubbub and hullabaloo. The whole town turned out to greet the sailors back from the sea.

But this one little boy named Toby had a father who was not a sailor. His father built big sailing ships.

And every night he came home to his little boy. He told Toby stories that began, "Once upon a time, when I was a sea captain. . . ." He took his little boy for walks along the shore. And he tucked his little boy in bed.

All that was fine. Toby and his father were the best of friends, long ago.

But one night when they were eating supper together, the father said, "I should like to go to sea on the fine big ship I'm building. . . ."

He said he would like to see the strange foreign

places again. "I'd like to see the whales," he said, "and the flying fish. I'd like to feel the deck rolling under my feet."

Toby thought about his father going away.

He did not like it at all. Big tears popped into his eyes.

"Perhaps I could go with you?" he asked.

His father looked at the tears. "Toby is only a little boy," he thought. "Only a little boy with tears in his eyes."

"No, Toby," he said. "Little boys can't go to sea."

Then the big tears rolled down Toby's face. His father sighed a little and patted the boy's head.

"I'll stay ashore then," the father said. "Never mind, Toby. I'll stay ashore."

But, do you know, at night the father would stand outside in the garden. He would listen to the sound of the sea and sniff the salt smell. He would walk up and down the garden path, rolling a little, as if he were on a rolling deck.

Toby saw him do it, night after night, long ago. He thought of all the stories his father had told him about the wonderful life at sea. And all at once, he thought how much his father must want to be a sea captain again.

So the next day, Toby went up to the attic.

He took his father's captain's clothes out of a big sea chest. He asked Lucy Hawkins (who kept house for them) to air the clothes, and she did.

"Could you press them, too?" he asked.

Lucy Hawkins said yes, indeed she could. She pressed the big blue coat and the blue trousers. Then Toby put the captain's clothes on his father's bed.

And that night, when his father came home and saw the clothes, he didn't say a word.

His eyes twinkled at supper, but he still didn't say a word.

The little boy waited and waited for his father to say something. When he was too tired waiting, he said, "If you see a whale when you go to sea, will you look at it very hard through your glass? Then you can tell me exactly how it looks."

Toby's father didn't answer that.

He said, "Who put my captain's clothes on my bed?"

And Toby said, "I did, sir. I wanted them to be all ready when your new ship is ready to go to sea."

He sat up straight and tall when he said it, and he smiled. Then Toby didn't look like a little boy at all.

"You're getting to be quite a big boy," said his father. He put down his napkin and stood up.

He took Toby up to the attic. There he opened a small sea chest. He took sailor clothes out of it and held them up. They were just the size for a little boy.

"These clothes were mine," the father said. "I wore them when I first went to sea."

"You were just my size!" whispered Toby.

His father nodded his head. Then he said, "Ask Lucy Hawkins to air them and press them, and put them on your bed. They'll be just the thing for you to wear when you go to sea with me."

Toby took the sailor clothes in both arms.

He smiled the happiest kind of smile and ran down the stairs, long ago.

And do you know, he rolled a little bit as if the stairs were rolling, too, on a ship at sea.

45

Seagulls

When you see cloud-white seagulls
  Sailing up the bay,
They make you think of rolling seas
  And places far away,
Strange adventure places . . .
  And then you want to be
A free and roving sailor
  Sailing on the sea.
When sailormen spy seagulls
  Flying toward their bow,
They know it means they're close to land—
  That any minute now
They'll sail into harbor.
  And then they're glad to be
Back from a journey
  And home from the sea.

Widow Harper's Spice Cake

NOBODY in Snug Harbor ever expected to see Captain Northeaster or the *Counterpane* ever again.

Everybody said, "Probably lost with all hands." And everybody was very sad about it.

"What about the Captain's five grandchildren?" whispered all the good women in the town. "Who's to tell them the *Counterpane's* lost?"

Nobody wanted to tell them.

"Oh, dear, dear, dear," thought good Widow Harper, "there must be some way to break the news to them gently!"

And then she thought she'd make them a big clam chowder. She thought that after they'd eaten a good, hot clam chowder—why, then she could tell them, and they wouldn't mind so much with their tummies all good and warm and full.

So Widow Harper made her best clam chowder and she carried it piping hot across the cobbled street to Captain Northeaster's house.

She knocked on the door, and all the five grandchildren—Tom and Tim, Tam and Tad and Arabella—rushed to the door to let her in.

"Well, now, dearies all," cried the good widow, "I've brought you a fine chowder."

All the grandchildren licked their lips.

"And now," said the good Widow Harper, "if you'll just sit down and eat clam chowder till ye can't eat any more clam chowder, then—I'll be much obliged."

All the grandchildren sat around the big round table and ate clam chowder. They ate a bowl each, and it tasted so good that their cheeks were pink and their eyes were shiny.

"Want more?" asked the good Widow Harper.

But the five grandchildren said, "No, thank you, Widow Harper."

"Sure you can't squeeze in a little?" she asked.

Tom peeped into the kettle and shook his head.

"We *could* eat a lot more," said Tim.

47

"It was so very good!" cried Tam.

"But there's just enough left for Grandfather," said Tad.

"And he should be in any time, now!" cried Arabella.

The good Widow Harper tried to tell them that Captain Northeaster was lost at sea.

She tried and tried.

But the words wouldn't come out.

So she smiled a thin smile and pulled her thick shawl around her.

And she went home.

"Oh, dear!" she muttered, and she sighed, "Oh, well!"

And then she had another idea.

"I'll make them a good steamed pudding. And after the steamed pudding, I'll surely be able to tell them!"

But after they ate the steamed pudding—she couldn't tell them.

And she couldn't tell them after the codfish cakes.

She couldn't tell them after apple tarts.

And she certainly couldn't tell them after cherry cobbler, which happened to be Captain Northeaster's favorite thing to eat.

Because every time the five grandchildren had eaten one helping of those good things, somebody said:

"There's just enough left for Grandfather!"

And Arabella said, "And he should be coming into port *any* time now!"

It was very hard on poor Widow Harper, cooking all the time like that, and running across the cobbled street, and knocking on the white front door of Captain Northeaster's house.

But at last, one day, she rolled up her sleeves and went into the kitchen again.

"Spice cake," she said firmly. "And after spice cake I'll tell them for sure."

She got out raisins and currants and eggs and sugar and flour and milk, and she beat and she whipped until her face was red. Then she slipped the cake into the oven and looked across the street.

"Spice cake," she said. "And then I WILL tell them."

When the cake was baked, light and fluffy, nice and spicy, the good widow pulled her shawl around her, picked up the steamy cake, and started across the street.

But she couldn't get across the street.

That steep cobbled street was so full of people running about and cheering and shouting, and so full of dogs barking and pigeons flying, and people

Mutiny

THE *Emily A. Bowsted* was sailing across the sea on a quiet night. Everything was quiet. Even the steady wind pushing the sails made hardly a sound.

And the whole crew of the *Emily A. Bowsted* sat on the deck whispering together. They whispered very quietly under the pin-point stars in the dark sky.

What they whispered was bad.

"Our captain should never have taken a woman aboard," the leader whispered.

"She's a very small woman," said one sailor. "And a very young woman."

"That's neither here nor there," the leader hissed. "Don't bother to tell me she got lost in a shipwreck, and our captain could hardly refuse to take her home to her parents. The thing is, a woman is a woman. And a woman is bad luck on a ship."

"Dreadful bad," an old sailor said. "Why, we might be boarded by pirates, or sunk by a twister, or dashed on a rock!"

"What will we do?" asked the crew, crowding closer together.

"We'll mutiny," the leader whispered.

He said they would meet on deck at dawn. He said they would wait for the tramp-tramp-tramp of the captain's boots coming up the companionway.

"We'll grab him and put a hand over his

mouth," said the leader. "We'll gag him and tie him and put him ashore on the first desert island—"

"And the little girl?" asked the crew.

"Nothing to that," the leader whispered. "She's too small to cause us any trouble. We'll put her ashore, too."

"Then away we'll go, safe from bad luck," laughed the old sailor.

And one stout sailor with a peg leg said, "Maybe we'll be pirates!"

The leader stood up tall and wicked-looking with his great black beard.

"Remember everything," he whispered. "We

meet at dawn at the top of the companionway."

"Aye, aye, sir," whispered the crew.

Away they crept like shadows in the shadows on the dark deck.

At dawn they came back. They tiptoed across the deck from all sides. They crouched at the top of the companionway and waited for the captain to come up.

They waited with hearts pounding.

They waited with eyes straining.

They waited and waited for the tramp-tramp-tramp of the captain's boots, coming up the stairs.

"Why doesn't he come?" whispered the leader.

Just as he said that the whole crew heard a

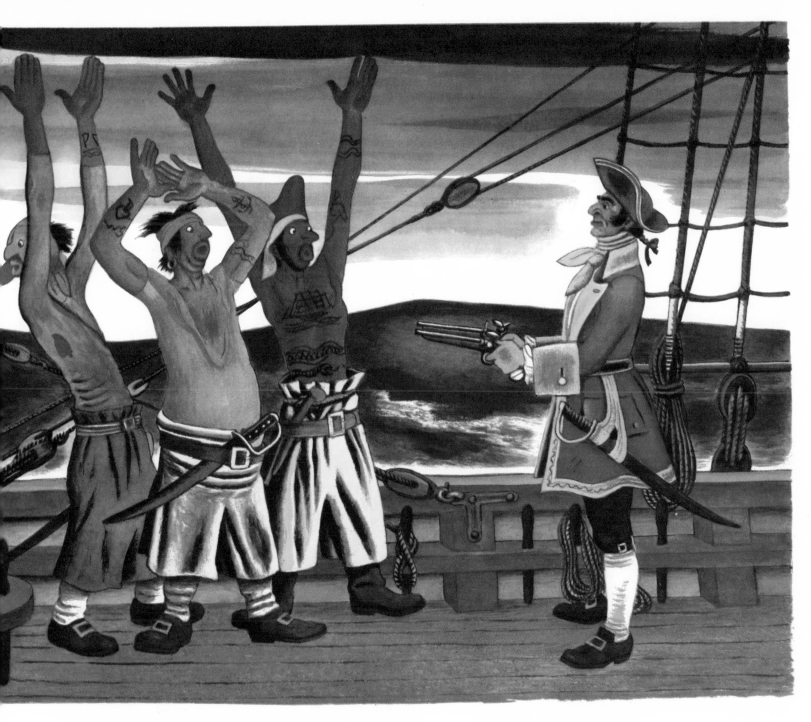

tramp-tramp-tramp from below. They all leaned forward, ready to grab the captain the minute he came up.

Closer and closer came the tramp-tramp-tramp.

When it sounded on the stairs, the leader said, "Ready now!"

And just at that moment, a firm voice behind them said, "All right, mutineers! Put up your hands!"

Those mutineers swung around with their hands over their heads. Their eyes began to goggle, because there was the captain, right on deck with two pistols in his hands!

Who was making the tramp-tramp-tramp?

Who was coming up the stairway in the captain's boots?

They peeped around each other's shoulders in great surprise.

Tramp—tramp—tramp! And a little girl came out on deck with big boots on her feet, and her arms full of handcuffs.

"Now, madam," the captain said. "Please handcuff this mutinous crew all together."

The little girl did.

She handcuffed one mutineer to the next, and so on all around the companionway.

Then she fastened the end handcuffs to the mast.

And there was the whole wicked, mutinous

crew in a helpless ring, and angry as angry bees!

"How did you know our plans?" they growled. "They were secret plans. Nobody but us was supposed to know!"

The captain didn't answer.

Neither did the little girl.

They went up to the bridge to steer the ship.

"Where to, sir?" the little girl asked.

"First," said the captain, "we'll dump this crew in jail at the nearest port. Next, we'll get a loyal crew. And then, madam, we'll take you home to your father and mother."

The little girl sighed.

"You have no first mate now, Captain," she said. "Don't you think you need some kind of first mate until you get a full crew together?"

The captain chuckled. "Indeed I do. I need the kind of first mate who keeps her eyes open. The kind who hides on deck when there's mutiny aboard, and who overhears the plans."

He chuckled again and put the little girl's hands on the ship's big wheel.

And the little girl stood up straight and tall in the captain's extra boots. For now she was the captain's first mate.

Then away went the *Emily A. Bowsted*, sailing on the bright summer sea, with the captain and the first mate singing at the wheel, and the whole wicked crew chained to each other, and grumbling and growling, and angry as angry bees.

LIGHTHOUSE

A little boy who couldn't sleep
    Sat tall up in his bed
And watched the lighthouse flashing
    Way out at Lobsterhead.

"When I am grown I'll keep that light
    As bright as any star
To guide the ships to harbor
    From journeyings afar!

"I'll live out in the lighthouse there
    Alone up on the rocks
And signal for provisions
    To the watchers on the docks.

"I'll fill the empty lanterns with
    The best sperm oil from whales,
And I'll polish up the windows
    With salty sea in pails.

"I'll keep the beacon gleaming out
    Across the stormy sea,
And all the ships will curtsy
    When they sail clear of me!"

But 'way out in the lighthouse there
    The weary keeper said:
"Someday I shall be sleeping in
    A quiet village bed!

"Then I'll pull great velvet curtains
    Around my bed so tight
That I won't hear the surf pound
    Nor see the beacon light.

"I'll go walking on the cobbles,
    And dine so full and well
With the fine chatty townsmen, I'll
    Forget the whale oil smell!"

But all throughout the stormy night
    The beacon threw its beam
Across the boy's small bedstead
    And through the keeper's dream.

And all the weary sailor men
    Steered wide of Lobsterhead
And its sharp rocks that jutted
    Up from the ocean bed.